Let's Go Fishing!

By Jan Wahl
Illustrated by Bruce Lemerise

A GOLDEN BOOK · NEW YORK
Western Publishing Company, Inc., Racine, Wisconsin 53404

Grandfather came to my room with fishing tackle and gear. He wore tall rubber boots and a weird hat with furry feathers.

"Are we going fishing?" I wanted to know.

"If you get dressed soon," he answered, shifting his feet. "Grandmother has made some cheese sandwiches."

So we drove to the cold river. The sun was just coming up. We got out our fishing rods.

"Let's dig for worms," Grandfather said. He found thirty-two worms, and he was the winner. I found only four, because I liked to watch them wiggle and crawl.

"I can't fish with these," I told him. "They are my friends."

"Then we will use mine," Grandfather decided. His worms were limply waiting to be hooked. "Oh, well, we will use the cheese from the sandwiches," Grandfather grumbled.

He showed me how to throw a line far out in the blue river. But my line got caught in a chestnut tree. We climbed the tree and unhooked the sharp hook.

An old lady came by with a little girl. They both carried binoculars. "We are bird watchers. What are *you*?" asked the old lady.

"Fishermen," Grandfather sighed. We slid down the tree. I scuffed my shins on the rough bark.

"Let me give you a Band-Aid," volunteered the old lady. Actually, I needed six Band-Aids. She got them out of her big cloth knapsack.

"Find any birds?" my grandfather asked.

"I saw a grackle," the old lady answered.

"I saw two sparrows," the little girl spoke up.

"Did you find any *fish*?" the old lady asked.
Grandfather only coughed.
"We found a lot of worms," I boasted.
"Do you eat worms?" the little girl asked. Grandfather coughed some more. We all said good-bye.
I put new cheese on my hook. This time Grandfather threw my line out beautifully.

Grandfather threw his line out, too. We sat on the moss bank, silent as two stones.

A sleepy badger poked his face through the leafy underbrush. A frisky raccoon skittered out from the reeds and stood studying Grandfather and me.

After a while a man with ragged clothes wandered by.
"Are they biting?" he asked, friendly-like.

"No…" drawled Grandfather.

"But there's a mess of bass around. That's what they
tell me," the man said in a hushed voice, as if soon plump
bass might be leaping.

The man said, "Good luck!" and disappeared through a grove of pine trees. We heard him stepping on fallen branches and singing a loud song.

"Drat! That will scare the fish away," Grandfather complained.

I didn't want to tell him, but I was sure my cheese had fallen off the hook.

Some flies and a fat hornet found us and buzzed noisily about.

We sat, looking at the great cotton clouds rolling in the bright sky.

The hornet grew tired and *zimmed* off.

"I'm getting hungry," I said, wishing really hard the cheese wasn't gone from the sandwiches. We looked at the four empty slices of bread.

The old lady and little girl came by. "Did you see a black-capped chickadee?" the old lady eagerly asked. Her gaze swept through the air. She saw the slices of bread.

"What kind of sandwiches are those?" she asked. "Will you trade them for drumsticks and apples? We can put the bread out for our birds."

We made the swap.

We propped up our fishing rods with heavy rocks. Our hooks were still unbitten. The sun felt hot. We kicked off our shoes.

We lay on our backs. Squirrels chattered.

Before we knew it, we were asleep. I awoke to find Grandfather shaking his head over the lines.

"No luck here," he muttered, very sad. "But we could go digging."

"For a family of worms?" I wondered.

"No," my grandfather said. "Before *my* grandfather's time—long, long ago—this was Indian territory. There might be some Indian things buried."

We made deep holes. The old lady and the little girl gave up their bird watching to watch us. "Are some fish down in there?" the little girl finally asked.

"No," my grandfather said, feeling foolish. He dug further, bringing out pieces of things that glittered in the sun—

> rocks with shining mica
> broken bits of glass
> squashed bottlecaps.

He handed each object to me.

Under the green earth, down in the yellow clay, he found an arrowhead. We whooped and hollered! Grandfather cleaned it till it looked fresh and new. You could smell the old times down there in the damp earth.

Grandfather came upon more arrowheads...part of an ancient warrior's necklace...a huge Indian pot with a crack in it!

We did an Indian dance around the treasures. The old lady and the little girl danced with us. We gave them each an arrowhead.

The afternoon was turning breezy. The wide river rippled.

The old lady and the little girl left. I tried to show the Indian pot to a family of brown rabbits. The rabbits hopped away.

The pot had painted figures of ponies running. When I held it, Indians seemed to lurk near every tree, log, and stump. Grandfather said, "The river had a strange name—Was-o-hah-con-dah."

Deer and turkeys and bears and foxes again roamed
the woods, again a thick green forest.

By shutting my eyes, I could see them.

There were Indian campfires, many campfires, sending
signals of magic smoke. I could taste the smoke.

Indians in canoes, six braves to each canoe, paddled up the Was-o-hah-con-dah. I could feel the pull of the paddles.

Indians on ponies galloped past the shore with strings of shells and pipes and tomahawks. I could hear the hoofbeats.

"We will not go home empty-handed. That is the first mark of a *good* fisherman," said Grandfather.

"What is the second mark?" I asked.

"That he be proud of his catch." We carried the things we had brought and the things we had found to Grandfather's car.

Grandfather leaned against the open car door, and he laughed.

"Is there a third mark?"

"Yes, that he know when to quit," he said with a wink.

Then I climbed in beside him, and I held in front of me the beautiful pot, and we drove home together.